KALI MA

Kali Ma

A Collection of Short Stories

El. T. Fullah

Aghori Publishing Press

Kali Ma: A Collection of Short Stories

Published by Aghori Publishing Press

Library of Congress Control Number: 2022950524

ISBN (paperback): 9781662935459
eISBN: 9781662935466

Contents

The Violinist's Concert

"Look at me!" the violinist shrieked. "Look at how well I play this violin! Look how fast I can play it and how many notes in succession I can achieve! Tell me how good I am!"

The crowd cheered, "You are amazing! We love you!"

The performer smirked, the validation and reverence filling the void between his low self-esteem and gargantuan ego.

"I am better than you, right?"

"Yes!" The crowd responded.

"You see yourselves as inferior to me?"

"Of course!"

"Do you want me, a superior being, to play more for you plebeians?"

"Please!"

"Well, you will have to do something for me. . . I need to separate my true supporters from those who have recently hopped on the bandwagon."

"We will do anything!" The crowd shouted in unison. "We will debase ourselves as much as is to your liking!"

The performer stood from his chair and set down his violin. "Kill the person next to you."

For several moments, the concertgoers stood paralyzed. Then several groupies in the front row began viciously scratching and clawing at their neighbors. The feral violence metastasized, and the congregation devolved into bloody entropy.

After the grisly deaths of approximately half of the audience, the violinist raised his hand.

The remaining concertgoers halted as commanded.

"Those of you who are still living," the violinist announced, "I bestow the glory upon you of being better fans than those you killed. You proved your worth to me. You have earned the right to keep hearing me play the violin."

The bloodied audience roared.

The violinist returned to his chair. Lifting his instrument again, the performer began peacocking his holy musical miracles once more to his most ardent devotees.

Idolatry

"What are symbols?" Rahul asked the fellow villagers who had gathered around him.

Above murmurs in the crowd, one villager responded loudly, "Symbols are representations of revered concepts."

Rahul scoffed. "What revered concepts did the Holy Tree represent?"

"The Holy Tree, which you desecrated, represents humility - the supremacy of nature over man."

"So why am I tied to this stake and about to be burned to death by my fellow men? Is nature commanding you all to murder me?"

The crowd remained silent.

"Don't you all see the insanity behind your idolatry?" Rahul asked the audience. "Not only 'holy' trees - other 'symbols' such as flags, statues, prayers, languages, aesthetics, temples, churches, or mosques. Anything revered is merely a vector through which humans of weak conviction can boost their egos and, in many instances, exploit weaker humans for power. If we ever wish to reach our full potential as a species, we must transcend idolatry;

we must always challenge everything we hold 'sacred' and strip it of any reverence."

"Enough of this heresy!" The village priest hissed, pivoting to the man who stood beside him. "Sanjay, I order you to commence the burning. Rahul must pay for disrespecting the Holy Tree."

Sanjay, a childhood friend of Rahul, reluctantly approached Rahul with a lit torch.

Rahul smiled at Sanjay. "Sanjay, so it will be you, my old friend, who ends my life in the name of idolatry."

"Rahul, why did you desecrate the Holy Tree?" Sanjay asked, his eyes swollen with tears. "You knew death was the punishment."

"I had to challenge idolatry. So be it if I die as a martyr for that cause."

Sanjay shook his head and dropped the torch onto the pile of embers surrounding Rahul's feet.

As smoke clouds began to choke the air, Sanjay muttered to Rahul, "You fool, don't you see that martyrdom is also a form of idolatry?"

Rahul's eyes widened as he burned alive.

Beware of the Charlatan

"I spoke with God last night," the Charlatan announced to his Church congregation. "And He warned me about the liberal conspiracy behind the geometric concept of Pi."

Darlene noticed her mother in the second pew, deeply entranced by the Charlatan's words.

"The idea that Pi is an irrational infinite decimal is a lie created by the Devil to undermine faith in God!" the Charlatan shouted. "Pi is 3.14! No more, no less! God does not create irrational infinite numbers! What God creates is perfect!"

"Amen," the Church congregation muttered.

The Charlatan pivoted on the dais to face Darlene, soaking wet and suspended upside down by her feet from the Church ceiling.

"My sweet Darlene," the Charlatan began. "I know you are in there somewhere, afraid and confused. Don't worry; this will all be over soon. Once I exorcise the demon from your body, you will again be free."

Darlene whimpered, "What is wrong with you? I'm not possessed!"

"Is Pi an irrational infinite decimal?" The Charlatan whispered.

Darlene hesitated.

The Charlatan pressed a hot poker into her cheek.

Darlene shrieked in pain.

"Is Pi an irrational infinite decimal?" The Charlatan repeated.

"Mother!" Darlene cried, "Please end this madness!"

Darlene's mother mumbled, "Father Donald said God spoke to him. Therefore, if you contradict Father Donald, you contradict God."

"Is Pi an irrational infinite decimal?" The Charlatan barked a third time, shoving the burning poker into Darlene's exposed armpit.

"It, it... equals 3.14!" Darlene cried.

The Charlatan smiled. "Louder."

"Pi equals 3.14!"

The Charlatan faced the Church congregation. "Did you all witness how God works through me? I have succeeded in casting out the demon from our beloved Darlene."

The Church congregation clapped.

"The Devil hunts our youth," the Charlatan continued. "He intends to turn our children against us. And only I can save you like I saved Darlene here this morning."

"Glory to God!" the Church congregation shouted.

The Charlatan approached the pews from his dais. "For our next service, bring me your children who doubt God, and I'll cast the Devil from them. . . For a fee, of course."

"How much is your fee?" One church congregant asked. "My son doesn't believe you won the presidential election, so I fear for his soul."

"For you, Mr. Watson, I'll charge $100. You can make the check out to my super PAC."

"God bless you, Father!" Mr. Watson shouted.

The Charlatan pointed at one of his altar boys. "Hannity, boy, come here and change my diaper. I've been walking around in my feces all morning. Do you expect me to change my own diaper? Jesus Christ."

Across the Universe

One morning in 2019, NASA astronomer Farah was diagnosed with late-stage cancer. That afternoon, a NASA satellite received a peculiar radio signal from space.

The radio signal was a discernible rendition of "Across the Universe" by the Beatles, which NASA beamed into the cosmos in 2008. However, while the notes and composition were identical, the instrumentation was complex, almost discordant, and otherworldly.

Farah asked herself, "Does the extraterrestrial entity behind this radio signal understand music? If so, how does it interpret music?"

Farah and her team beamed into space a simplistic tune conveying generic happiness.

Three months later, a NASA satellite received an alien musical composition conveying generic sadness.

Farah asked, "Does this alien entity understand music's connection to human emotions? Does itself harbor a similar emotional spectrum?"

Over the next few months, Farah and her team sent progressively intricate and complex music compositions of all genres conveying increasingly nuanced, and even conflicting, emotions. The alien entity replied to each composition with a perfectly inverse version. And its response time shortened with each communication, from weeks to days to several hours.

Beneath the fascination with extraterrestrial communication, Farah understood a problematic truth. The shortening response time indicated that the alien entity was rapidly approaching Earth.

However, blinded by the novelty of interstellar interaction, Farah instructed her team to keep conversing with this alien entity. Besides, Farah figured, "the speed of the alien entity approaching Earth is far quicker than any human defensive response can be."

The response time went from one hour to one minute. To ten seconds. To -

There was a knock on the door at Farah's work facility.

Farah opened the door.

A little girl stood outside. She handed Farah a cassette tape and ran away.

Farah played the tape for her team. The otherworldly music on the tape was the most beautiful musical composition ever produced. It encapsulated the full human emotional spectrum in a single melody. So overwhelming was the alien music that after the tape ended, several team members immediately killed themselves with whatever objects they could find nearby. Others instantaneously devolved into psychosis, with one person shrieking that he was now God.

Farah was the only one who remained alive and held onto her sanity. "I'm going to destroy this tape," she declared. "We can never let it get out. It would drive humanity to madness."

Some months later, on her hospital death bed, Farah asked her brother to rummage through her apartment closet for a yellow box. In the box was a letter Farah had recently written claiming how she, as a lifelong scientist, was excited about her death. The letter concluded with, "How can we claim to understand our death if we can't even comprehend ourselves in life?" Beneath the letter was a tape.

Farah's brother returned to the hospital with the letter and the tape. Farah listened to the alien music once more on headphones as she entered the next phase of her journey.

The Empathy Development Experiment

"Good morning, Dr. Singh," the Psychology Research Coordinator said. "I'm told an unfortunate incident occurred recently in our Empathy Development Research Program. Please fully debrief my colleagues and me on this matter."

Dr. Singh nodded and began his PowerPoint presentation. "As you know, my research focuses on developing empathy in violent offenders who show no signs of remorse for their actions. Last year, we developed a simulation program in which convicted murderers would vicariously experience a virtual regeneration of their committed murders from their victims' points of view. This program would simulate the victims' physical and emotional sensations as well. We hypothesized that this program would help violent offenders develop empathy and remorse."

Dr. Singh moved to the next slide. "Our first test subject was William F., a convicted murderer who brutally stabbed his girlfriend, Kelly, to death.

"The virtual simulation went smoothly. William experienced Kelly's murder from Kelly's point of view. He felt her pain, anger, sadness, and desperation."

Dr. Singh switched to the third slide, which contained a security camera video of William in his cell by himself. Dr. Singh did not press play yet.

"I do not have a concrete explanation for what happened later."

Dr. Singh played the video in fast forward. He had seen the graphic video too many times, so he primarily focused his gaze on the ground.

The audience remained silent during the first portion of the video. Then some gasped, others averted their eyes, and one man exited the room.

As the video continued behind him, Dr. Singh explained, "My working hypothesis is that after the vicarious virtual simulation, William failed to disassociate himself from Kelly's experience; William continued to believe he was Kelly. And once William's manifestation of Kelly realized she was in the body of her killer. . . well. . . How he got a sharp object into his prison cell, I don't know."

Dr. Singh turned and glanced at the video, knowing the worst was over. The footage was showing the prison janitorial staff cleaning up the pools of blood and vomit and removing sliced-off fingers and toes, slabs of skin, and intestines from the ground.

"As you can see," Dr. Singh said, "I have my work cut out for me."

The Anti-Incubus

"So, Caleb," Dr. Lee began. "Tell me about this recurring dream you've been having."

18-year-old Caleb, under the influence of an experimental MDMA drug used on patients suffering from post-traumatic stress disorder, began mumbling. "It starts on the same day, my tenth birthday. We are all gathered in the backyard. I'm opening presents. The first two presents are normal action figures. The third present is. . ." Caleb paused.

"Take your time," Dr. Lee said.

"The third present is a severed human head. My severed head."

"And then what happens?"

"I look around the party. I'm surrounded by people I don't recognize, and they are all dressed in black robes and pointy hats. They start chanting."

"What do they chant?"

Caleb began trembling. "Needles. Knives. Needles. Knives. . . They come closer. And closer. . . They start stabbing me. And then I wake up. . . But when I go back to sleep, it's the same dream all over again."

Dr. Lee nodded. "Do you remember your actual tenth birthday party?"

"Yes."

"Did anything bad happen that day?"

"My friend broke one of my action figures. Beyond that, it was a normal birthday party."

Dr. Lee raised an eyebrow. "My fourth-grade teacher put me in timeout one time unfairly. But I never experienced nightmares about that. It isn't normal for past trivial matters to manifest into recurrent horrific nightmares. . . So, Caleb. We are going to run some functional MRI scans tonight to observe your brain activity while you sleep. Does that sound good?"

"Okay."

That night, in the MRI control room, Dr. Lee and his colleagues observed a fast-asleep Caleb being fed into the MRI machine from behind a glass panel. For the first two hours, Caleb's brain activity appeared normal on the imaging computer screens.

Around midnight, Dr. Lee began to observe unusual brain activity.

Then one of Dr. Lee's colleagues screamed. Dr. Lee looked forward.

Standing beside the MRI machine was an inhuman figure donned in a black robe and thin pointy hat.

"Call security!" Dr. Lee shouted instinctively. "Make sure he doesn't leave the room!"

The white porcelain figure turned to Dr. Lee, its coal-black eyes connecting with Dr. Lee's. It grinned. And then vanished.

After sending Caleb back to the psych ward, Dr. Lee spent the night's remaining hours reviewing camera footage with hospital security guards and police to figure out how someone could have entered the secure room.

Once morning arrived, Dr. Lee was so exhausted from the night's events that he momentarily fell asleep in a chair in the MRI control room.

Within moments, he found himself in a shadowy dungeon, hanging upside down by hooks pierced through his feet. In front of him stood his fourth-grade teacher Mrs. Watts, dressed in a black robe.

Mrs. Watts hissed, "Looks like timeout wasn't enough for you, huh? Now I'm going to have to punish you with needles and knives."

The Snuff Film Artist

Once upon a time, an Artist lived in a warehouse apartment near a bustling city.

The Artist directed and starred in (without revealing his identity) "snuff films," videos depicting the Artist murdering kidnapped victims creatively. This hobby was the sole activity that pushed the Artist's heart rate above 70 beats per minute.

One night, the Artist found himself perusing his dark web "snuff film" page. An individual with the username "A Client" had commented on the Artist's most recent upload: "How can I contact you? I need your services and will pay well."

The Artist smirked. He had never had a client before.

He sent the Client the following direct message:

"Send a full frontal nude picture of yourself to the email address below, so I know you're not a cop." The Artist provided the secure email address.

Some minutes later, the Artist received an email notification and saw that the Client had complied with the Artist's request.

"Good," the Artist whispered. He now knew the Client's appearance.

The Artist emailed the Client the following instructions:

"Tomorrow at 10 am, visit the men's restroom in Central Station. Go to the left trash can and drop off in a blue plastic bag $8,000 in prepaid debit cards, each card holding $1,000, and your target's information in a folded notecard. I will be one of the thousands of men who will enter the men's restroom after you leave."

The following morning, the Artist spied from afar as the Client entered Central Station and proceeded into the men's restroom. Minutes later, the Client emerged from the bathroom and disappeared into the frenzied morning crowd.

After waiting ten minutes, the Artist retrieved the blue grocery bag from the restroom and returned expeditiously to his warehouse lair. Inside the grocery bag were eight prepaid debit cards and a folded notecard.

The Artist unfolded the index card, his pulse monitor watch flashing 67 beats per minute.

The card read: "You."

The Artist pivoted and saw the Client and two men in skull masks standing behind him.

They had followed him home.

The Artist woke up still in his apartment but chained to a metal chair and gagged.

Before him stood the Client and the two masked men, one of whom aimed a camera at the Artist.

"You murdered my sister," the Client shouted over the heavy metal music blasting from a nearby stereo. "And now I'm going to get sadistic on you. Don't worry; I'll post this video on your blog."

The Artist giggled internally. His pulse monitor watch flashed 80 beats per minute. Wow, he thought. A new record.

I'm Going To Rob You

I promise I'm a nice person.

But hypothetically, what if I wasn't?

At an upscale bar, I overhear you bragging to your friend about how much of your net worth you have invested in crypto. "I will forever HODL," you say.

I see the bartender's register screen when he closes your tab. I hear you both converse for a minute. You have a unique name. Good.

I find your address on one of several data aggregating sites.

I find your house and follow your movements.

The next night, you're drunk again in the town, and your ride-share service driver is taking too long to arrive. "Hey, sir. I'm available," I say, pretending to be a gypsy cab driver. "I'll charge half of what your ride-share trip will cost. Come with me."

Usually, in express kidnappings, the criminal will take the victim at gunpoint to as many ATMs as possible to withdraw as much cash as possible.

Fuck an ATM. I simply ask you via gunpoint to log into your crypto wallet on your phone.

Okay, what if I can't get to you?

Easy. I find your social media. You think you're smart because you set your Facebook settings to private. But what does your public profile picture show? Is that a photo of you, your wife, and your son? What is on your son's sweatshirt? His school name?

How much money is your son worth? I film my masked self shooting both of his kneecaps. Using an anonymous email account, I send you a muted version of the video, so you can only imagine how loud he is screaming.

You comply with my demands because you believe you can recover your money later. You read on the news that the US government can track down and recover stolen cryptocurrencies.

Except I'm not an idiot who holds my received ransom money in crypto. I immediately send the ransom money to a puppet anonymous crypto wallet of my friend who lives outside of US jurisdictional reach. My friend converts the crypto to fiat and hides the stolen cash in prepaid debit cards. I then disappear with my friend.

I can do this to you. But I'm a nice guy. So you're good for now. But maybe you should stop talking about your cryptocurrency portfolio in public. You never know who is listening.

The American Dream

Vlad spent 2017 traveling throughout the American northeast, searching for a home in which to stake his claim and build his American Dream. He found a perfect candidate in the blue-collar town of Transylvania, New Hampshire.

There, he envisioned a parasitic campaign to suck every last drop of blood from the town.

Vlad manifested a scheme with a local physician, Dr. Szilágyi, in which Dr. Szilágyi would overprescribe oxycodone to patients suffering from pain brought on by manual labor. Whenever the doctor grew "concerned" with a patient's growing addiction to opioids, she would ostensibly cut off the patient from oxycodone and then, for a kickback payment, "refer" the patient to Vlad for further "prescription fulfillment".

And once Vlad and his minion parasitic dealers introduced heroin to these initial desperate patients, the fate of Transylvania, New Hampshire was sealed.

Together, Vlad and Dr. Szilágyi turned Transylvania, New Hampshire from a bustling blue-collar city into their ghastly opium den, a HIDTA filled with soulless eyes, terminated jobs, desperation, broken families, abandoned children, and lost hope.

As a result, Transylvania, New Hampshire's property value plummeted, attracting the attention of real estate company Nosferatu Properties.

The CEO of Nosferatu Properties met with Vlad and Dr. Szilágyi.

"I seek to build New Hampshire's most gaudy for-profit drug rehabilitation center here in this town," the CEO of Nosferatu Properties expressed. "However, drug rehab centers need patients, so I've approached you two. Dr. Szilágyi - if you can expand your private practice beyond the town of Transylvania and recruit more doctors, and Vlad - if you could cut your heroin with more fentanyl, enough to make people zombies but not kill them, then I will award you both significant stakes in Castle Rehab Facility."

Vlad and Dr. Szilágyi agreed to the venture. And that night, all three celebrated their new business deal with bottles of spiked blood.

Vampires had once again struck gold in America.

The Human Zoo

Youssef exhaled a cloud of marijuana smoke and handed the bong to his friend Abdul.

While Abdul hit the bong, Youssef asked, "Hey, Ab. What if. . . life is like some simulation?"

Abdul choked as he scoffed out his own smoke cloud. "What are you talking about?"

"I'm serious," Youssef said. "What if life is like some reality television show? And you're the main character but don't know it?"

Abdul shook his head. "You're an idiot, bro. You think you are so important that someone would make a show about your life? Fuck outta here. The fact that you even asked that question reveals a lot about you. . . "

Youssef scowled. "It was just a question, bro. Chill."

"Don't tell me to chill. 'Oh, I'm living in some Truman Show!' 'Life is a dream, and everything I've ever experienced is in my own head!' Bro, do you know how narcissistic you sound? You think everything around you, the whole world, this couch on which we're sitting, this house in which we're hanging, my whole self, all exist to, what, bolster your narrative of your life?"

"Bro, relax. Take another hit-"

"It's not only your dumb ass question that frustrates me, Youssef. Humans for millennia have been concocting senseless narratives which place themselves at the center of existence. Take religion - 'oh, God, the creator of everything, cares about me, Abdul, so much that He actually listens to my prayers and watches over me!' Astrology - 'stars millions of miles away conspire to influence events in my infinitely singular life - whether I meet my next girlfriend today or get a parking ticket. . .' 'Everything in life happens for a reason!' 'It was fate!' Fuck that! We are here randomly, and nothing fucking matters! There is no God, no astrology, no destiny, and definitely no fucking TV show in which we're living!"

(Cue The Human Zoo theme music)

Coming up on the next episode of TV's longest-running reality show, The Human Zoo: The Life of Abdul. . .

Youssef, our paid actor, will continue to drop hints about the truth of Abdul's reality to Abdul. How will Abdul respond? Will he further lose his grip on sanity? All that and more next week! Stay tuned, folks!

An Act of Intimacy

One afternoon, Manuel decided he needed to reinvigorate his marriage. A crevice had burgeoned between himself and his wife Griselda over the past few weeks, and Manuel wanted to address whatever the underlying issue was honestly.

He sauntered onto the ranch house porch where Griselda was lounging in a rocking chair reading a magazine.

"Griselda, put your magazine away for a second. Let's do something fun. I feel we have been growing distant over the past few weeks."

Griselda avoided eye contact with Manuel. "What are you thinking of doing? I'm too tired to have sex, Manuel."

"Let's smoke this marijuana I have. I bought a magical strain today at the dispensary."

Griselda paused. "What makes this strain magical?"

"It is supposed to build intimacy between whoever uses it."

"Like ecstasy?"

"Not exactly."

Manuel settled on a bench beside Griselda and packed a bowl with the magical marijuana. Igniting the weed, Manuel exhaled a cloud of smoke and handed Griselda the bowl.

Hesitating first, Griselda eventually took a hit.

Several rotations later, Manuel began studying Griselda intently.

The strain worked as advertised; Manuel could peer past Griselda's melting defense mechanisms and into whatever thought Griselda was suppressing most.

"I don't know what's wrong with me," Griselda suppressed. "For the past few weeks, I wake up unimaginably hungry every night around 3 am. I stare at Manuel and fantasize about eating him. Last night, I grabbed a knife from the kitchen to slit Manuel's throat. Thank God I stopped myself. But I don't know if I'll have the strength to stop tonight."

Manuel smiled because Griselda was finally making eye contact with him - she was reading Manuel's most suppressed thought:

"I know Griselda wants to eat me. I am awake every time she wakes up at 3 am and whispers to herself about devouring me. Why won't she do it? I want her to. It would be an act of intimacy in the most literal sense; we would become one entity, and our marriage would be forever solidified."

Griselda bit her lip, her eyes swelling with tears. "Are you sure, my love?"

"Yes," Manuel responded. "Let's do it tonight. . . I love you so much, my Griselda."

Old Friends

Jeremy did not expect to see Helena that evening at the grocery store.

"Helena, is that you?" Jeremy asked, his heart pounding as he tapped her shoulder.

Helena's two young sons fled behind her legs as she pivoted to face Jeremy. Her face ignited. "Jeremy! Oh my God!"

They briefly hugged.

"I can't believe I'm seeing you here," Jeremy said. "How have you been?... I see you currently have a family."

"I do," Helena said, beaming. "I've been married for about eight years. Are you married?"

"I am right now," Jeremy responded. "Have been for about ten years. I have three children, eight, seven, and two. They are wonderful."

"I'm so glad you are doing well, Jeremy."

"I as well."

Both Jeremy and Helena fell silent.

"You know, Helena, I was so in love with you."

"I know, Jeremy. I loved you too. It's a shame that life separated us."

"Would it be appropriate to ask if. . . you know, we see each other again? Strictly platonically, of course."

Helena pursed her lips. "Um… Sure, why not? My husband George is taking the kids to his mother's this weekend. I'll be free Saturday night."

"Great. I should be free then as well. I'll tell my family I have business travel."

Jeremy and Helena exchanged cell phone numbers. As Helena trailed away, Jeremy heard Helena's older son ask, "Mommy, who is he?"

Helena replied to her son, "An old friend, dear."

That Saturday night, Helena and Jeremy found themselves strolling in the park they had frequented years earlier.

"Do you harbor any regrets about us?" Helena asked.

"Of course," Jeremy said. "We were so passionate about each other. And we never were able to fully explore our young love, the purest kind of love."

After some silence, Helena asked, "Do you want to sleep together tonight?. . . You know, get a small taste of what life could have been like for us?"

Jeremy paused. "Helena, I don't know. We both have separate lives and families now."

"We can sleep together platonically, like you said. I want to lay with you one last time before we continue our regular lives."

Jeremy smiled. "Okay, I can do that."

Retrieving a shovel from Jeremy's car, Jeremy and Helena began digging into the ground till they reached their shared coffin. Unlocking the wooden casket, Jeremy and Helena climbed into the empty space and lay together in each other's embrace.

"Only for tonight," Helena muttered, interlocking fingers with Jeremy's hand.

Jeremy kissed her forehead.

Adjacent to the excavated burial site, the gravestone read, "Here lies fiancé and fiancée Jeremy Reston, born 1813, and Helena Douglass, born 1814, both tragically stolen from this earth in a house fire on July 16, 1834."

A Village With Only Men

I hated women. They had ruined my life. A misogynist? Incel? I gladly accepted those labels.

My fellow MGTOW (Men Going Their Own Way) friend told me of this village in remote India where only men lived. Sounded like my type of place: men being men doing man things. No cunts within to manipulate or torment me.

Accompanied by a local English-speaking tour guide, I decided to visit this remote male-only utopia.

Upon arrival, I witnessed several naked men praying to a giant phallic structure, a Shiva Lingam, which the tour guide explained was the Holy Penis that created the universe. Interesting.

And as promised, no women were seen. Good. No cunts.

That night, I ventured from my lodge with my tour guide and saw something appalling: seven male duos, one older male and another in his early twenties, were engaging in anal sex around the Shiva Lingam.

What the fuck?

"What is this gay shit?" I asked the tour guide.

"Gay?" The tour guide responded. "I don't understand what gay means. What you see is our normal holy nightly ritual."

I left the conversation alone.

The following morning, I roamed the village with the tour guide.

"How do you people reproduce?" I asked him. "I know men are being born into this village. The population has been consistent for generations."

The tour guide explained, "To reproduce, we steal nonmales from neighboring villages and inseminate them. We keep the male babies and discard the nonmale ones. Once we get a nonmale to produce a male heir, we sacrifice the nonmale in a Sati-like fire to the Shiva Lingam. It rids the village of nonmale pollution."

Holy shit.

Before I could ask another question, the tour guide said, "Come with me. The village leader wishes to meet you."

The village leader, a highly effeminate elderly man, resided within the Shiva Lingam. His genitals rested on a golden platter, and his pubic hair was immaculately groomed. Around him were six young men of all races except white.

"Hi Fred," the village leader said in English. "I hope you have enjoyed your stay thus far in my village."

"It's been interesting, sir."

"You will be happy to know that I have chosen you to be my seventh Penis Caretaker."

"What? I'm not a homosexual, sir."

The effeminate man giggled. "Homosexual? I hold no concept of sexuality. Our anal penetration ritual is a holy prayer to the Shiva Lingam, to masculinity itself. What is more manly than the natural dance between domination and submission? Do you have testicles or not?"

"I do."

"Then be a man and submit to my penis...I sense hesitation. It would behoove you not to resist."

The tour guide struck my head with a brick. The last thing I remember was the effeminate man muttering this prayer, "Glory to masculinity and dominance. May the Shiva Lingam forever protect us from the impurities of estrogen."

Patrick in Paradise

I devoted my entire lifetime to God, and upon my death, He blessed me with promised entry into His Kingdom.

Once in paradise, I indulged in every desire I had abstained from in my earthly life: sex with men and women, drugs, gluttony, and music. Everything my slut daughter had enjoyed on Earth despite my repeated warnings of damnation. Par for the course, she died before me from a drug overdose. I had to confirm her identity during her autopsy, the first time I had seen her since her early twenties.

One day, I met a fellow holy man named Shay. After having sex, we lay in bed together and pillow-talked.

"Is it just you who made it here from your family, Patrick?"

"Correct. I was the only one in my family who took God's word seriously. It's a shame, really."

"It is. You get to enjoy all these divine pleasures by yourself."

I paused. "That's true. If only I had done more to turn my family toward the right path. Especially, my daughter."

"I'm sure you tried your best."

"I. . . kicked my daughter out of my house when she came out as a lesbian."

"As I would have done, too."

"I did love her and prayed for her soul every day. . . especially when she died. But how was I supposed to respond to her unGodly ways? She would have corrupted my soul if I accepted her perverse crimes."

"That's true. You wouldn't be next to me if you did. You would be suffering eternal torture with her."

I half-smiled. "Is it really that bad? You know, down there?"

Shay laughed. "She is undergoing torture beyond your worst imagination. It serves her right."

I swallowed. "Does she really have to spend eternity being tortured? I don't think her crimes justify that horrendous of a punishment."

"Why do you care? You followed God, and she didn't."

"I care. . . because I'm still her father. I raised her. Despite her sins, I don't wish her to be in pain."

"You are overthinking. Enjoy God's gifts. You've earned them."

Why was I now feeling anxiety and guilt? I thought God was supposed to reward me with peace.

Shay then rose from the bed and started putting on his clothes. "I'll talk to you later, Patrick. We have an eternity to get to know one another. We don't have to rush it."

"Well, nice spending time with you, Shay. . . I didn't catch your surname. What was it, again?"

"Tan."

"Well, let's do this again soon, Mr. Shay Tan."

Identity Crises

Lyla had developed multiple identities by the time she reached early adulthood. Growing up a middle-class woman in an upper-class community, Lyla learned as a survival adaptation to switch between personas to best assimilate into whichever environment she found herself.

Among rich folk, Lyla adopted a superficially "cultured" dialect lest she was thought of as not "elite" enough.

Lyla channeled a street-savvy persona among her extended middle-class family, lest she was thought of as "too rich."

Among her conservative friends, Lyla suppressed her more liberal opinions.

And vice versa.

Among her cannibalistic cult friends, she pretended that she harbored no doubt about the holiness of consuming raw human meat on a full moon.

Among her dead friends, she purposefully avoided sensitive subjects such as birthdays and anniversaries lest she was thought of as "too alive."

However, Lyla felt most comfortable alone at home.

Every night upon returning to her abode, Lyla would ecstatically unzip her human costume and scamper over on her 100 spindly legs to her gargantuan spiderweb-like trap in her basement. There, she would cherish her moment of solitude while feeding with her forty pincers on the latest human captive who had wandered into her dwelling.

Ancestors

I died at age 65, and the powers that be granted my wish to join my ancestors in the cosmos.

I wish they hadn't.

Afterlife has not been what I expected.

The first surprise of my afterlife was that "the cosmos" was The Cosmos: Inn and Bar, a dingy walk-up hotel located in midtown Manhattan, New York.

The second was that my ancestors and I barely understood each other. We all spoke period-specific versions of our languages and had different cultures around communication, which often provided for confusing and frustrating dialogue. For example, when I first arrived at The Cosmos lobby, I made the mistake of waving "hello," and half of the room believed I was casting an evil spell on them and began ululating.

The third surprise was that I was physically the oldest ancestor, having died at age 65. It appeared that all of my ancestors had died when life expectancy was much shorter. As such, I was called "Grandpa" by those who were literally the grandparents of my grandparents.

Shit - where is my nightgown? Suleiman and Abraham - those little Black Plague-era shits. They are these fucking twelve-year-old twins, perpetually existing in the awkward phase of early puberty. They are whiny and emotional, their voices crack, and they find it hilarious to steal my belongings and burn them. They must have stolen my nightgown. Again.

Then there is Boris, who died as an infant. And Boris is a feisty baby, crying at all times during the night. Every night. And pooping. For eternity.

How can I forget Cleopatra? The disgruntled former Queen of Egypt has ranted about how the current generation is the worst - for 60 straight generations.

Why the hell did I do that mushroom-filled yoga retreat in the Arizona desert in 1981 and pray to join my ancestors upon death? This shit sucks, man. I don't recommend it.

The Politician

(*written in early May 2022*)

One Sunday morning after Church, the Politician had lunch with his wife and daughter in his upper-class suburban home.

The Politician's wife said, "I am so elated that God has finally redeemed America by revoking Roe v. Wade."

The Politician clasped his wife's hand. "Yes. We are recalibrated as a country. Once Roe v. Wade is overturned, I will introduce legislation outlawing abortion in all cases, no matter what."

"Hallelujah," the Politician's wife replied.

The Politician's daughter fumed. "But, Father, aren't you being hypocritical? Didn't you pay our former maid to have an abortion last year?"

The Politician stiffened. "It was a moment of weakness, and God forgave me."

The Politician's wife added, "The Devil seduced your father with that temptress-"

"Silence!" The Politician roared at his wife.

The daughter again challenged, "But, Father, don't you realize outlawing abortion makes every woman a target of any man who wants to terrorize women? What if someone forces himself on me and impregnates me? How could you make me carry that baby to term? Don't you care about my rights as a woman?"

The Politician scoffed. "Honey, outlawing abortion is about something much bigger than so-called women's rights."

"What is it, then?"

"It's about reversing white genocide."

The daughter raised her eyebrows. "Explain, Father."

The Politician smiled. "Honey, over the last half-century, the Godly order upon which America was founded - wherein Whites ruled and Blacks served, has been under assault by Jews and homosexuals who want to see Whites diluted, Blacks liberated, and America turned into a third world cesspool ruled by the United Nations. And our enemies have been succeeding. White birth rates are declining, homosexuality is rising, miscegenation is widely accepted, and third world immigrants are invading our country and reproducing like rats to backfill the population gaps."

"So revoking Roe v. Wade fights back against Jews and homosexuals?"

"Yes, honey. It will result in more White children. We need all the white children we can get, regardless of the reproduction circumstances. And while I don't particularly care for Blacks, we need them for labor purposes, as God intended. By forcing low-income Black women to carry babies to term, we ensure they will not spend time and resources climbing the economic ladder. Their only option for income is to labor for us.

"And while liberal states continue to promote abortion and homosexuality, their populations will decline, and ours will rise. In one or two generations, we will have completely reversed white genocide and reestablished God's order."

The Politician's wife exclaimed, "Amen-"

"Silence!" The Politician growled. He turned to his daughter once more, "Does that make sense, honey?"

The daughter paused. "I never thought about it like that. It does make sense. We can't give up this country to non-White people. Race comes before gender."

The Politician beamed with an evil smile. "I'm glad you understand now, honey."

Life in Blue

Penelope was twenty years old when she confessed to her parents that she could not see the color blue.

Her father presented her with a picture of a solid blue square and asked, "What do you see here, Penelope?"

Penelope responded, "A dark green? Purple?"

"Penelope must suffer from blue-yellow color blindness," her parents concluded.

But Penelope knew that wasn't true. She could adequately distinguish red, pink, green, yellow, and purple.

Furthermore, already a social outcast among her peers, she resented that she had yet another quality that set her apart from mainstream society.

In her junior year of college, Penelope spent hours at the library studying colors. She discovered she was not alone in her lack of perception of blue. The color blue was in fact a relatively recent invention in the human lexicon. Historical texts from ancient Greece, India, Iceland, Arabia, and other societies never once mentioned the color blue. The only ancient civilizations to have cultivated a sense of blue were those in Ancient Egypt and Peru.

So when did the word blue become this widespread color?

One answer was in 431 CE when the Catholic Church began to ascribe colors to saints – the Church gave Saint Mary a blue robe.

Penelope's curiosity was not satisfied, though. She had come across too many unanswered questions in her research.

One night, Penelope visited one of her university's labs which contained spectrophotometer equipment. Using a controlled flame as a light source, Penelope deployed one machine to isolate the flame into separate color wavelengths. The machine projected only one narrow portion of the flowered color spectrum for the user to observe through eyepieces. Looking directly into the eyepieces, Penelope adjusted the machine's knob to focus only on the area of the color spectrum deemed "blue."

Penelope spent several minutes staring deep into the supposed color which had evaded her perception her whole life. "So this is pure blue," Penelope whispered to herself. But the color still appeared purple.

She then noticed something unusual. The purple color began to morph. And turned utterly black.

"Congratulations on finding me, Penelope." A voice hissed.

"You have been hiding in the color blue this whole time?" Penelope asked calmly, her eyes still on the machine's eyepieces.

"What better way to hide than in plain sight?"

"I have to tell my world the truth."

"No one will believe you. And soon, you won't even believe yourself."

"Why is that?"

A sharp pain flashed through Penelope's skull, forcing her to close her eyes. She shrieked, retreating from the ocular lens.

She tripped over her lab chair and fell onto the floor. Once the pain subsided, she opened her eyes. And the only thing she could see was the color blue.

The Nature of Fear

What about me frightens you?

Is it my elongated human-adjacent body structure?

My transparent glass eyes? Or my veiny and bloody scalp, from which hang several long strands of black hair?

What about my serene voice? The mere fact that I can talk? Does my speech frighten you?

The truth is you are not frightened of me at all.

You are frightened by your assumptions of me. You do not understand me, so your worst imagination develops wild notions about how threatening I am to you.

You assume that if you leap out of your bed and sprint for the door, I will scamper down from your ceiling and snatch you.

You assume that if I have you in my grasp, I will dismember and devour you like a feral predator. Or I will take you to my family, who will then flay you alive in some supernatural ritual.

Now, indulge me for a moment. Ask me what about you scares me.

I fear you, not because I do not understand you, but because I do.

Your baseless assumptions about me offer me insight into exactly who you are.

And I am terrified that you will ultimately kill me.

I refuse to let that happen.

Tonight, I will kill you first.

Here I come.

www.ingramcontent.com/pod-product-compliance
Lightning Source LLC
Chambersburg PA
CBHW031543060726

47590CB00004BA/1490